# The Baby in the Hat

# THE BABY IN THE HAT

◄ • an early romance • ►

*written by* Mr. Allan Ahlberg

*with illustrations by* Mr. André Amstutz

WALKER BOOKS
AND SUBSIDIARIES
LONDON · BOSTON · SYDNEY · AUCKLAND

My Best Friend caught a Baby
In his Hat.

*It's true!*

The Baby's Mother gave him
Half a crown.

He spent the money
On a Railway Ride.

Got lost in London,
Oh, the Fog was thick,
Fell off a bridge
And landed in a Ship.

Sailed down the river

To a Stormy Sea.

Became a Cabin Boy

And then — a Mate.

Engaged with Pirates
In the Southern Seas.

*Hurrah!*

Served Good King William's Navy
'gainst the French.

Then Home at last
With Treasure in his Trunk.

He walked that Street
Where he had caught the Baby,
A different, grander Hat
Upon his Head

And saw a smiling Face
Up at the window

And gave a Little Gasp ...

And fell  in Love.

His Bride — she was that Baby,

Did you Guess?

And now they sail
The Southern Seas together

With Loyal Crew and Baby

... of their own.

It's true!